EGG MONEY

Ronald Wheeler

EGG MONEY

Ronald Wheeler

Parson's Porch Books

Egg Money

ISBN: Softcover 978-1-936912-67-4

Copyright © 2013 by Ronald Wheeler

To order additional copies of this book, contact:

Parson's Porch Books

1-423-475-7308

www.parsonsporchbooks.com

Parsons Porch Books is an imprint of Parson=s Porch & Company (PP&C) in Cleveland, Tennessee. PP&C is an innovative non-profit organization which raises money by publishing books of noted authors, representing all genres. All donations from contributors and profits from publishing are shared with the poor.

Table of Contents

Proctor

It started around the age of eight. "You must start watching what you eat," his mother said. "I can see you have my sluggish metabolism." He also had his mother's dark hair and her soft complexion. The two of them ate large lunches together; mounds of mashed potatoes and pasta of all kinds. At supper they nibbled at salads and raw vegetables. All the while Proctor eyed the cookie jar, the breadbox and the refrigerator. Wasn't that good his mother would say. In six years you'll be in high school and you won't make the team if you're too fat. Football was long in the future; Proctor existed in the here and now. He would go to his room and wait for everyone to settle into their evening routine and he would sneak back into the kitchen, make a sandwich, tuck it inside his shirt and go outside or into the bathroom to eat it.

Most of this deception was for Proctor's father, who was a former semi-pro football player and maintained his playing weight. He often came home tired from long negotiations, and bourbon put color back into his cheeks. At dinner he often said to Proctor's mother, "give him a little steak, he's a growing boy and needs protein. That rabbit food won't put muscle on his body."

His mother's voice would become tense and she often said, "If he has steak he shouldn't have desert, after all, his diet..."

"Why couldn't he have both," his father would say and punch him playfully on the arm.

In high school Proctor had two good friends and they often went to the slate dump and searched for blasting wire and unexploded blasting caps. Angelo fashioned a device to run wires in parallel and out to the blasting caps. Then when he turned the handle each in turn would explode. It was as loud as a .22 caliber long rifle bullet. They imagined themselves as Hollywood directors filming a World War II epic.

Proctor was fascinated by Sydney Greenstreet and Charles Laughton and never missed a picture they appeared in. He wondered why they were fat. He knew why he was fat. He was Proctor, God made him this way. His friends could eat anything and remain skinny as fence rails, but what about Greenstreet and Laughton? Did they eat as recklessly as old Father Sopar, who came to dinner and ate everything at least twice or did they try to lose weight? Proctor imagined them going about hungry and angry and thinking of food, and then going home and eating a huge sandwich with lots of mayonnaise and peanut butter. Mostly, however, Proctor believed they didn't put themselves in such agony; they were fat because they chose to be fat. He could see it in their faces, they didn't eat on the sly, no, they relished food as he did. His sneaky trips to the kitchen when he was eight became a ritual of deception and pleasure. He was a furtive eater of salami. Even his two friends didn't know his secret. Father Sopar told Proctor he was just right. When they served communion Father told him to remove his pants before putting on the robe. After service Father would massage his buttocks and sometimes his genitals. Proctor didn't like the attention, but put up with it because Father said he would have him removed from choir if he didn't cooperate. That all changed when Proctor's voice changed and his body coarsened. His perfect pitch evaporated and he was requested to join the men's choir. But he could no longer carry a tune and failed to show up for practice.

Proctor's public image was one of self-denial. He passed up all the comfort foods when eating with his two friends at school, and put nothing more than salad on his plate. No one saw the rolls of salami he had stashed behind a wall in his closet. He didn't think of himself as deceitful, he really believed he was dieting when out in public, because he forgot about the rolls of salami his grandfather had made. One night, his friend Mario said, "You're lucky Proctor, you don't know what I go through to hide my pipe smoking from my mother." Proctor looked at him with a mysterious smile: he ached to be home in bed with a big chunk of salami. He didn't need another vice he already had one that was destructive.

Proctor's two friends: tall, skinny, pimply faced Mario and skinny Angelo with his towering intellect graduated and went their own way. Mario never dated in high school because of his appearance. Angelo made girls feel uncomfortable with his intelligence and he never dated much either. Angelo had a stroke before earning his Ph. D in philosophy at the University of Michigan, where he met a Spanish physician. They discovered insatiable passion and made love in the library, on the beach and even on busses. Mario took a series of lovers. He would lie in their arms and tell them how he hardly dated in high school. He'd had an unpleasant appearance and had been forced into the weekend company of a neurotic smart ass and a shy fat kid. A lot had happened to them and they never thought of Proctor anymore.

Proctor's father sent him off to a fat farm to get his weight under control before he started college. The only thing those six weeks did was intensify his hunger for salami. That fall he went to college and continued to expand his waistline. He would lie in bed and eat garlicky salami as the smell permeated the room. "You can eat it front of me, you know," his roommate Alex said. "You don't have to wait for lights out. I don't mind."

They were dorm mates for four years and each fall moved back into their old room amid much backslapping and camaraderie. Neither boy enjoyed being home for the summer. Proctor didn't like it because of all the patronizing looks. Alex didn't like leaving all his girlfriends behind.

In the winter of their senior year Alex fell in love and wanted to share his happiness with Proctor, who had not dated all through school. "If I help, will you go on a diet?" Alex asked.

That night Proctor ate the last of his salami and tossed out his supply of bleu cheese. The next day they rented an apartment sized refrigerator and stocked it with non-fat yogurt, lettuce, steaks and chicken.

While Alex went to the cafeteria Proctor walked the Diag and suffered the constant pangs of hunger. He had small portions of steak or chicken breasts and fish. Slowly the pounds came off. When he went home for Easter he was down to 276 pounds and by summer was down to 250. Just thirty pounds short of the goal he and Alex had set.

Proctor spent a lot of time in the pool at the Clubhouse. There he met a lifeguard name Hillary, who was tall and muscular and had the metabolism of a piranha. She cooked wonderfully smelling dishes full of garlic and spices and ate them with gusto as Proctor nibbled on carrot sticks and steamed fish. Their relationship deepened and they married. Proctor worked hard at providing a good life for them. He made a lot of money and went deeply in debt to buy a house.

Hillary got pregnant as planned after five years of marriage. In her last trimester Proctor watched her eat enormous mounds of mashed potatoes and it made his stomach ache. He remembered those days of sneaking off with a huge sandwich stowed beneath his shirt.

Hillary gave birth to a healthy boy and quickly began to lose the weight she had gained. For his part Proctor had rediscovered the fat boy always just beneath the surface. Even though he had lost a lot of weight he always felt fat. He looked in the mirror and saw his warm, brown eyes looking back—the eyes of a poet. There was loose flesh under his chin and arms, but his legs were pleasantly plump. He slowly began eating all the forbidden food, especially salami and began to regain the lost weight. His mother voiced her concern about his weight gain and so did Hillary.

One night he brought a plate of salami, blue cheese and crackers and milk as they watched television. Hillary said, "didn't you have enough for dinner?"

He ignored her.

"You're gaining weight, a lot of weight," she said. "And it's all fat. You know that thin men make a lot more money. If you keep putting on the pounds you'll never get a raise and we'll never get a bigger house.

He wrenched off a huge piece of salami and stuffed it in his mouth just as he used to before Alex guided his diet.

"You never used to eat salami," Hillary said. "It's all going to go to your hips you know. I never married a fat man. You need to go back on your diet."

At every meal they fought about Proctor's addiction.

"Look at you," she said. "Scarfing down meatballs like a starved person, for Christ's sake. You're really starting to gain weight fast. I feel it each night you get in bed. Your side goes down and mine goes up."

"Well," Proctor said. "You never look sexy any more, coming to bed with all those rags on. I never thought I married Raggedy Ann. You never want to get close any more."

"I couldn't get close if I wanted to," she said. "Look at yourself." "You're mean," he said. "I never knew how mean you were."

Later, when she was asleep he took some of his Grandpa's homemade salami to the bathroom and stood eating it in the dark. He flipped on the light and looked in the mirror. He saw a familiar face looking back that reminded him of the old Proctor—the fat Proctor, the content Proctor.

Every day now Hillary raged about his weight. She really believed they were arguing about his weight, but it really was about Hillary—the tall, muscular woman, who had married a slimmed down version of a fat Proctor.

In a final act of desperation, and perhaps guilt, Hillary offered to help Proctor. "I'll eat the same things you do," she said. "I can live very well on carrot sticks and steamed fish.

In her face there was no compassion, no determination to help, just dispassionate discourse—lip service on her part and Proctor knew it. The worst years of his life were living on that diet and his stomach had ached ever since. He went upstairs and packed, taking care to gather all the rolls of hand-cured salami, one of which he tore in half and began eating as he carried his bag out to the car.

Egg Money

When I was growing up, in the 1940's, I spent summers on the family farm in Kentucky. I was young and of little use except to do some ginning, as they called hauling water from the well to the field hands while they put up hay.

There was little opportunity to make money. The nearest neighbor was more than half-a-mile away, and they had a passel of kids to help with the chores. So I was pretty much left to my own devices, which meant doing nothing and taking all day to do it.

Usually my second day I traipsed off to Harris' country store and bought a year's supply of penny candy, which I ate in one day. Then for something sweet I resorted to eating mushmelons. They were delicious, especially when picked dead ripe early in the morning with the dew still on them.

Dewberries were another favorite. There weren't enough of them to make a pie, but enough for a light snack.

Later, when apples started ripening I had my pick of the orchard: Grimes Golden, Rome Beauties and Mountain Boomer among others. I relished the "Boomers" because they were as large as softballs, and (I think) because they were inaccessible. They grew on a tree so high they couldn't be harvested. My grandfather named the tree "Mountain Boomer" when it appeared the tree would grow to more than forty feet tall. The only way I could get an apple off the tree was to throw dirt clods at it until I knocked one down. Then I had to catch the falling apple so it didn't get bruised. My efforts were always rewarded with a delicately flavored apple that would last most of the day.

One day while picking a delicious red raspberry snack in the garden a Rhode Island Red hen worked her way out of the briars flapped her wings and made a lot of noise. On my hands and knees I followed her path into the briars and discovered what she was so proud of A nest of grasses filled with eggs. I quickly ran to the house and told my grandmother about the discovery. She said they do that all the time, and that they were getting ready to set—hatch out some baby chicks. She said she should keep the chickens up but she just didn't have the heart. She told me to gather the eggs and she would give me half to trade at the store.

I located a split oak basket and made my way back into the briars. Before I finished I had found two more nests and a total of 37 eggs. My grandmother gave me 19 and she put the rest in her egg crate ready for market.

I now had my hot nickels; they were brown and round, and, to my eyes, worth their weight in gold.

The country road followed a nearly dry branch for most of the way. There were large areas of bedrock where the stream in times of high water had scoured the stone clear of soil. It made for a solid road for the farmers and their wagons, but it blistered bare feet. Where the roadbed was sandy I spied snake tracks as they squiggled across the road in search of a drink. I wondered how they did it without getting blistered?

Harris' country store was about 12 by 15 feet. Its board and batten construction of rough sawn Pine lumber had weathered to a dark brown.

Large knots oozed sap that congealed in long white streaks down the sides. I learned not to touch the sap; it was nearly impossible to remove. Outside a small porch abutted the front of the store and a Sassafras pole supported a cast iron bell. A pull on the bell rope and Mrs. Harris slowly waddled her way to the store. She would arrive all red-faced and gasping for breath and fumbling in her apron for the key.

That first whoosh of trapped air was the most heavenly of smells. Today I would pay just to have that door opened on a hot day. The rush of air had a certain aroma I have never found except in that store and others like it. It had the scent, which is classical in every country store, and by which such a store could be identified blindfolded in any part of the country. It is compacted of many aromas and made into one, which is very light and fruity and yet more subtle than it can seem in analysis. These are its ingredients: Aromatic pine lumber, wide boards of it super-heated in enclosed air. The aromas of tobacco, the smoking, chewing and dipping versions, and the savory smell of un-ground coffee beans that never delivered in taste what its aroma promised. Last, but most important, was the smell of gum and candy that formed the upper register of the composite aroma.

There is one other special scent, very dry and acrid. It is somewhere between the odor of old newsprint and a country sick room, in which after a long illness, and many patent medicines, someone had died. The room had been purified with burning sulfur, and yet the odor of dark brown medicines, frail-bodied sickness and open-mouthed death still remained in the stained wallpaper and in the bedclothes.

All these scents overwhelmed my sense of smell for a few moments. I stood there and breathed deeply. Soon the rush of air was over and I entered.

At any given moment the store housed horseshoes and nails to attach them, flour, corn meal, pinto beans, fabric (mostly gingham), tomato soup and a lot of Carnation condensed milk. There also were some canned meats, chief of which was Red Devil deviled ham, which I always bought along with a ten- cent box of crackers that I ate on the walk home. On a shelf behind the counter was a display of patent medicines in small brown bottles. I didn't know what ailments they were for except I had seen some of them on night tables beside the very ill, so I thought they were mostly for dying people.

The glass display case contained the objects of my desire. Lined up like stalwart sentinels were packages of Clove, Teaberry, Black Jack and Juicy Fruit gum (in the green striped package). The lower shelf contained Baby Ruth, Mallo cups, Oh! Henry, Milky Way, Butterfinger, Mars, Almond Joy and assorted selections of hard candy.

I learned not to buy the chocolate candy bars. In the heated air of the store they turned to brown mush. I bought Butterfingers.

The perfume that poured out of that small store had great nostalgic power. I have only to encounter a scent wafting past on an unfelt breeze to be carried back in memory to a time when my only responsibility was self-gratification, and to a childhood that was inherently simpler and happier than I suspect most children enjoy today.

Lord Jim

Every evening on their daily walk Lord Jim paid little attention to Grady. He trotted along at the end of his leash, but seldom strained to chase rabbits as Grady had seen other dogs do. Sometimes Lord Jim looked back, one paw raised, tail extended as if on point, but the mournful look as he turned his head left Grady irritated. He would have liked a dog with more gumption, more spirit. Even after he filled Lord Jim's dish the dog would stare at him waiting for an invitation. "Dive in," Grady said, or "it's there, yum, yum time."

Grady often wished he had named the dog Muffin or some such benign name. He certainly didn't live up to the regal "Lord Jim." Grady had chosen that name from the way the Greyhound had posed: so erect and serene, as he made his selection at the shelter. All of the dogs were former racing dogs and had been given up for adoption to the shelter. Tucson had a large and active dog racing association so there was never an end to the supply of dogs. They used to be gassed until adoption agencies took over. Lord Jim, who had been trained to chase a dummy rabbit, hardly moved faster than a slow walk when they were out.

There was no mistaking what kind of dog he had. When they passed other walkers someone would invariably comment, "Oh! Look! A Greyhound.

An elderly gentleman they encountered nearly every day always exclaimed in a loud voice, "Too much leg. Not enough dog."

"An ancient dog. You know there's hieroglyphic evidence of these dogs thousands of years ago. Did you know that? Asked another senior citizen in baggy shorts, white socks halfway up the calf and an "I'd Rather Be Surfing" T-shirt. His expression was solemn and his tone as impersonal as Anthropology 101. "Yes, ancient dog. Ancient dog."

"You're probably right," Grady said as he glanced at the night lights that came on, their circles of light spaced at specific intervals between the Texas Rangers and the Bottle Brush plants. Tucson had a dark sky ordinance in effect and no outdoor lights could be installed without a shade casting the light down. The lights, small as they were, still illuminated the occasional remains of a dog's relief. "Fudgies" as one lady called them when she wrote to their newsletter.

"I just don't know too much about dogs," Grady added.

She was pleasantly plump with dyed blue hair, too much makeup and reeked of that cheap, spicy perfume senior citizens used. She had one of those rat dogs, as Grady termed them, in tow. It was a noisy and nervous Maltese that skittered from side to side on the sidewalk. Such dogs made Grady nervous. She had a musical and infectious laugh that made Grady want to accompany her for a few minutes. He noticed she had a large diamond on her left hand and even her dog had a diamond-studded collar. He wasn't looking for either a nurse or a purse, but being retired and widowed was a lonesome place to be. That's why he had taken others advice and adopted Lord Jim.

He had a living arrangement the year before, but the lady refused to consider sex and refused to cook. She stated clearly she had retired and all of her body went with her. Grady, though, seventy-one already, wasn't ready to give up on living, and when the need arose he merely made a trip across the border to Nogales to one of the many brothels there. Never being able to persuade the lady *friend, whom he called* Boxcar Bertha, to cooperate he moved out.

Suddenly the small Maltese turned on Lord Jim and all Grady saw were long legs flying and a brown body wrapping itself around his legs. There Lord Jim peered around Grady's leg and shivered in abject fear.

"Dukey, stop that this instant!" he lady said as she cranked the leash handle. When Dukey was hanging in mid-air she stopped and apologized to Lord Jim, patting him on the head while Dukey waved back and forth and emitted strangling noises.

"His real name is Marmaduke," she said. "I call him Dukey for short. He's really not mean, he just sometimes gets carried away."

With that she turned and breezed off, her heavy haunches made the fabric of her pedal pushers undulate. She waved over her shoulder and said, "Have a nice day."

He unwrapped Lord Jim from around his legs and bent to pat his head, "Have a nice day? I get sick of that shit," he muttered.

They always included the Safeway store on their walks. Grady was addicted to Starbucks and their vast array of over-priced coffees. It was a convenient halfway point on their walk and he would sip while keeping an eye on Lord Jim just outside the door where he was tied to the dog-hitching rail.

Safeway installed the rail for the two thousand or so residents of Sunrise Acres, who all seemed to own at least one dog and some more. So ubiquitous were the presence of dogs that everyone took to calling the retirement community "Dogpatch." At the monthly meetings the most heated topic of discussion was the presence of dog shit everywhere. There was an ordinance on the books that clearly stated all refuse was to be picked up, but having no enforcement officers, residents simply ignored it.

Grady always carried Wal-Mart bags, which he merely turned inside out and picked up the deposit. He used Wal-Mart bags because he thoroughly disliked the store and their inhuman policies regarding their employees. He had heard they made them work overtime off the clock so using their bags, which he got from a neighbor was poetic justice.

Lord Jim made the walk home difficult. He always was afraid of traffic, among other fears. That's why Grady always circled around the backside of Safeway, but on the way home he always took the shortest route, which involved crossing at the light. When the sign said walk Lord Jim insinuated himself around and between Grady's legs and whimpered. It was such a cowardly sound that Grady always unwound the reluctant dog from his legs and carried him across the street. On the other side he set the dog down, gave him a sharp yank with the leash and fought an impulse to throw him out in traffic.

At home Lord Jim went about his nightly routine as if nothing had happened. He lay on his cedar chip bed; head between his paws, and watched TV. His only movement was the constant twitching of his eyebrows as he looked from the set to Grady whenever he changed position.

He always felt guilty after their walk. And when Lord Jim looked at him, Grady thought he detected reproach, as if he could read Grady's innermost thoughts. With a dog one was always alone and introspective in his judgments. You did something mean to it and it was like you had done it in front of the world.

Grady reminded himself that he knew nothing of Lord Jim's past. He knew he was born and bred for racing, but he didn't know if he had. He couldn't imagine a dog so fearful would actually chase a stuffed rabbit. Perhaps he had been abused when he refused to race maybe that's what made him so fearful. Whatever the reasons, Grady always returned to his own thoughts, to his own responsibility.

During the day Grady always went to the recreation center and soaked in the 100-degree heat of the pool where he joined the "Bobbing Circle."

Nobody, it seems, ever swam in the pool they just donned sunglasses and hats and bobbed around in circles. It relieved his arthritis and his circle of acquaintances always provided information and rumors about goings on. It was there he learned about pig ears. He took a side trip each day and purchased the treats. Lord Jim tore into them with a ferocity Grady had never seen.

It was Grady's way of apologizing for his crude behavior even though it was overcompensation.

He had selected Lord Jim because he had begun to feel lonely. Ever since he had walked out on Boxcar Bertha he had started to feel bitter and angry, with no one in particular, for getting older. When he felt his anger was about to take him down he began to count his blessings.

He was seventy-one, but that wasn't old the way it was old fifty years ago. He remembered when people looked old at fifty and when they retired they lived the actuarial allotment of 4 years and eight months. Sure he had triple bypass surgery four years ago, but that was a mark of distinction around Sunrise Acres. Not to have a huge scar from belly button to chin made one sort of an outcast. Besides he was more energetic now and his general health was really good.

And he was only seventy-one he kept telling himself. On his next birthday he would be seventy-two, which he contemplated with a sense of foreboding and dread.

He had much time to brood over the past and he often sat in the rocker with the lights off as a numbness of spirit washed over him. It manifested itself in little fits of pique he had often seen in some of the most elderly people. He noticed that there was entirely too much skin showing. God gave us clothes to cover up the ugly, not to move to a warm weather retirement community and take them all off. Knees were especially ugly all wrinkled and knobby and women with their layers of fat drooping out from beneath their shorts made him nauseous.

There was one guy, who wore a thong that wasn't big enough to contain his penis let alone his testicles, which always seemed on the verge of breaking out. He was about eighty-two, and had no body worth revealing.

Why couldn't he keep his balls to himself? If he wanted to wear one of those skimpy thongs wear it in the privacy of his own home. There, at least, his bony legs and knobby knees wouldn't destroy the appetites of the ladies at their high tea or whatever. Even when he was playing poker with the guys the bony old fart came in, in defiance of the cover-up rule and wandered through the complex oblivious. He apparently was proud of his leathery skin and emaciated appearance, which made him look like an Egyptian mummy.

It enraged Grady. Why couldn't the bag of bones at least wear a towel? What he did was invade everyone's privacy with his bony ass and baldhead. In fact, Grady could barely tell the difference. It really was an invasion of privacy, but everyone did it today: sex on busses, peeing in elevators, flossing in the airport terminal, nudity and partial nudity everywhere, no one, it seemed, knew what privacy was anymore.

Lord Jim was fun. Grady bought a rubber rabbit from the thrift store, and he and Lord Jim spent hours in the back yard playing a tug of war. Later, Jim would plop himself down, head between his paws and fix Grady with a steady gaze. When Grady noticed and stared back he felt as if he was being drawn in to a world, an awareness of which he was unable to name.

One summer day, while taking their morning walk, Lord Jim began whining. It was a high keening wail and continued until they walked out of the wash. It was then that Grady saw the body, at least the legs as they protruded from beneath the Mesquite tree. He called 911 and waited until they arrived and pulled the body out—it was bony ass man

For the rest of the day he felt guilty for harboring bad thoughts about the old man. After all, he was somebody's father-husband-son and he didn't deserve a twenty-two bullet in the back of the head Mafia style.

The execution reminded him of his own mortality and he took Jim for a walk and stopped in the Horseshoe Bar after pushing a reluctant Jim into the dog enclosure.

Grady downed several Margarita's and felt perfectly fine until he stood to go. That's when the Tequila took full effect. He could barely stand and then only while walking backwards. He felt as if is eyelids were drying out and the roots of his hair hurt like a million tiny pinpricks into his scalp.

He managed to get outside and headed home with Lord Jim in tow.

At the traffic light, as they were preparing to cross, he heard a squeal of tires and a loud thump followed by something moving perilously close until it stopped against the light post. The car had barely missed him but had flattened the front half of Lord Jim, who lay as he was hit between Grady's legs.

Grady went home to an empty house. He unlocked the door and called "Jim!" Then he remembered. "Oh, shit..." he said aloud.

His walkout on Boxcar Bertha echoed in his mind. She was, after all, a nice woman: kind hearted, generous and full breasted. He could have stayed with her, sold his own house, and lived happily. What does sex matter anymore anyway? It's just an exchange of bodily fluids and very little at that.

As he reached for the phone to inquire about another Greyhound it rang. It was Boxcar Bertha. She hadn't heard about Jim, she was just calling to say how lonely she was. Grady held the pig ear up to the light so that it glinted off the Incised tooth marks Jim had left.

"Bertha I'm glad you called because I needed to talk to someone. I had a dog. Lord Jim. He got killed by a car tonight."

"I'm sorry Grady. I didn't know."

"How could you it just happened a short time ago. Say, we never talked about it, but do you like dogs?"

I love dogs. They're the best kind of people."

"Want to tag along and help me pick out another Greyhound?"

"I'd love to. Give me ten minutes to dress," Bertha said.

Captain Jack

Captain Jack appeared one winter Saturday in 1940.

In his darkened upstairs bedroom eight-year-old Lenny flew his imaginary Spitfire in a cockpit assembled from his grandmother's treadle sewing machine, a discarded broomstick and a fleece-lined replica of a fighter pilot's helmet. This was his Saturday night routine as the drunken arguments intensified. With the straps tightly fastened beneath his chin red hair stuck out beside his freckles. Occasionally his mother came upstairs, made some over-solicitous remarks, and then sat and stared out the window for hours. The bruises didn't show until the next day.

Lenny withdrew more and more into his fantasy of flight. All week he worked oh his stick and paper airplane models and read the information booklets provided, which helped him plan his sorties. He especially liked the European Theater because the German pilots seemed more formidable. He might accompany a flight of Wellington bombers part way on a raid to bomb Nazi installations—Lenny called them Nayzee's—or, as was usually the scenario, he operated as a lone wolf and stalked targets of opportunity.

He chose the Spitfire because of the deep, powerful throb of the Rolls Royce Merlin engine and the rounded wings, which presented a menacing yet strangely sensuous image. Each flight began with a full throttle climb through dark, heavy clouds into brilliant sunshine. Then Lenny throttled back, adjusted trim and settled comfortably into his seat and enjoyed the solitude of his world.

One Saturday night the violence from the kitchen penetrated the closed door and reverberated through his bedroom like waves upon the shore. He concentrated harder and harder on his attack of a flight of Heinkel bombers. He slashed right and left cutting huge arcs in the sky around the slower flying bombers. He was just ready to dispatch the last one when he thought he heard a voice. He bore in for the final kill; flew close and closer until the torrent of tracers tore the starboard engine apart and the Heinkel bored a hole in the English Channel.

"Well done," the voice said.

Lenny sat there momentarily stunned. Then he removed his helmet and stowed it carefully in a drawer of the sewing machine. He turned and there on the bed sat a freckled-faced, red-haired apparition in uniform.

Chills cascaded down Lenny's spine.

"Ain't nothin' to be afraid of," the apparition said, and then it slowly reclined on the bed, propped its head on one arm and fixed Lenny with a lop-sided, disarming grin.

"Who...who are you?" Lenny stammered.

"Captain Jack Nichols RAE"

"Royal Air Force?"

"That's correct. Something ain't it?"

"But how did you get here? I didn't see a car drive up or anything." "I just came. You needed me and now here I am. That's all I know." "But I don't need anybody. Besides you'd better be gone before my mother comes up here."

"She couldn't see me, only you can."

"Then you...you...you're a ghost aren't you?"

"You want me to be a ghost?"

"No. I don't...I don't want you to be...I didn't do anything wrong. You're not a constable are you?"

"Of course not. You can see me can't you? I'm Air Force. At least I was. The last thing I remember was a loud explosion, my cockpit filled with smoke and now I'm here with you. I can see you're uncomfortable so I won't stay long. I'll be back next Saturday, maybe sooner if things go crazy around here. Toodle for now."

Lenny looked forward to Saturday with a mixture of apprehension and expectation.

Captain Jack did return and he returned many Saturdays in succession. At first his visits were brief, but as Lenny came to accept him a genuine friendship developed. They spent many long hours together and Lenny would tumble into bed tired and happy.

On their Saturday night flights they discussed armament, engines, combat tactics and everything associated with the rugged but beautiful Spitfire. Lenny shared his knowledge with his classmates. His attitude changed from a sullen, morose, anxiety ridden third-grader into a confident and self-assured young man. His teacher requested he make a presentation on the Spitfire at assembly. He asked Captain Jack to accompany him

"I would like to but I can't," the Captain said. "You see I can only return here. This is our place, right here in this room. In fact, it's the only place I'm allowed to visit."

"But nobody could see you so how would they know if you went? Can't you do it just this once—you know, sneak off like I do," Lenny pleaded.

"It's impossible. You'll do well, but you mustn't tell anyone about us. It's our secret OK? Here's a tip: Pick out someone in the audience and talk to that person—nobody else—just that person and you'll do well. Gotta go now."

The day after his presentation Lenny came home to find the sewing machine and most of the furniture had been sold. The next day they moved to a smaller house. He built a new cockpit from wooden orange crates, but for a time things were quiet on Saturday nights and the Captain didn't return. Then three weeks later the arguments began anew and resounded even louder now that the house was smaller.

Lenny was just completing his pre-flight instrument check and as he started to rev up his engine he felt a warmth, a familiar presence, Captain Jack had returned. He smiled that disarming lop-sided grin and placed his hand over Lenny's on the joy stick. Lenny smiled at the Captain and together they took off and climbed through dark, heavy clouds.

Daisy

Fog, night breath of the mountains, gathered in the sharp-creased valleys and descended. It drifted past porch lights and blurred them, it settled over traffic lights and grayed them and it, without so much as a whisper, shrouded the buildings. It crept in before midnight and entombed the town.

Norman tried to pierce the fog with concentration. He turned the windshield wipers to full, but they screeched. He turned them back and slowed down.

The fog had appeared suddenly and frosted the windshield. With it came a cold, penetrating clamminess that smelled of old river bottoms and decay. Occasionally Norman could make out a ghostly window-framed light. A traffic light made an abrupt appearance and he barely stopped in time. The light perched atop a cast iron pole on the sidewalk. Next to it a mailbox stood sentry duty. A neon sign beckoned.

It was a typical small town bar: a pool table where two elderly patrons played a desultory game of eight ball; a shuffleboard with its corn meal dressing stood unused; and the ubiquitous juke box blared out Teresa Brewer's "Till I Waltz Again With You."

"What kin I git fur ye?"

"Bourbon and water," Norman said.

"Ya passin' through?"

"Yeah, but the fog's so thick. Do you think it will lift soon?"

"Well Sir," the bartender said, trying to hitch his pants past his ample

belly, "I don't rightly know, but most times it don't clearoff 'til mornin'." "Any good motels near?"

"Only good un' is the Daisy Cabins. That's near five mile outta town."

"Nothing in town huh?"

"Nah."

"I'll have another," Norman said as he slid his glass across the bar. "That's another 35 cents bud."

"At these prices one could nurse a really cheap hangover couldn't he?"

"Yep, but ya don' wanna." He walked toward the end of the bar and gave his pants another double hitch with no visible success.

Norman, warmed by the bourbon, settled back in his chair and surveyed the bar. The coral and green decor belied its fifties heritage. Everything fit, including the picture of Eisenhower above the bar. Next to it hung a curious poster. It appeared to be modeled after the Uncle Sam recruiting posters. It had a picture of an indistinct policeman with his hand extended. Only the finger was in sharp focus. Beneath it read "Drunk Drivers Don't Drive in Daisy." It was signed Joe Mann.

The ambiguity of the message prompted Norman to ask about it. "Oh! That. That's Joe Mann's idee alright," the bartender said.

"Well, if it's Norman idea he must have designed the poster didn't he?"

"Lord no," the bartender said indignantly, "why he's th' sheriff"

"Oh! I see. Then the Sheriff administers the program, is that it?"

"Nah, fur's I know he just puts 'em in jail."

Norman had been in the bar for more than an hour and the two elderly pool players had yet to take a shot.

"Those guys take their game serious don't they?" He had to shout the question a second time to be heard above the blaring juke box.

"Yep, they been at that game fur years."

"Don't they ever take a shot?"

"Yep, when they've a mind to. What'd you say your name was?" "I didn't," Norman said, "but it's Norman. Norman Lesko."

"Lesko. Lesko. Nah, can't say I ever heerd of it." He wiped the bar several times with a grayed, dingy cloth and added, "but I bet they's lotsa names I ain't ever heerd of ain't they?"

He walked over and inserted another house dime in the juke box. A few more drinks and several repeats of "Till I Waltz Again With You" and Norman decided he preferred the fogged-in loneliness of the road to the strange isolation in the bar.

As he rose to go the bartender broke his silence to state the obvious,

"Ya leavin'?"

Norman felt no need to reply and as the door slowly closed behind him he heard, "Ya should stay here."

The fog was still impenetrable. An involuntary shiver traced its way down his spine as the dampness hit him. The mailbox stood its lonely vigil, like a mourner. Norman gave it a thump and it responded with a hollow metallic ring.

The road ahead was invisible. Norman hung his head out the window and watched the left front wheel to keep it in the center of the road. Even that failed as he crunched gravel at the edge of the pavement.

Two headlights overtook him. As the car drew abreast he could read DPD on the side. The driver pointed him toward the side of the road with a flashlight.

After administering some sobriety tests the officer brusquely motioned Norman into his cruiser and said, "We'll have your car brought in."

Within minutes they drew up to a squat stone building. A tall, deeply tanned man, every muscle taut beneath his olive drab T-shirt, met them at the door.

"Howdy bud, I'm Sheriff Joe Mann."

Norman's heart skipped a beat as he recognized the name. Before he could respond the sheriff grabbed him around the shoulders and ushered him into the dimly lit building.

"You're here by accident, bud. Pure accident, the same as me, but we're not going to keep you. Hell's fire bud, we're not even going to book you. We're going to sober you up and send you on your way by sun-up."

The Sheriff kept up the friendly patter as he steered Norman toward a high-ceilinged room. As he rummaged in a locker the Sheriff kept up his patter, talking over his shoulder and casting sideways glances at Norman.

"I don't know how you got here, but you're here and I've got to deal with it. You understand this place doesn't exist. Not anymore. And it hasn't since October 8, 1954. That's the year the government closed the gates on the dam and this town filled up with water. Now I got no idea what year it is where you came from but for me it's six hours before the water rises and that's how much time I've got to get you sober and out of here."

As he handed Norman a gray sweat suit and a pair of high-topped gym shoes he exhorted him to hurry.

"There ain't much time. Get these clothes on and we'll talk as we run. You can run can't you?

"Well, yes, but I don't...I uh." Norman tried to frame a response but the Sheriff cut him off abruptly.

"It's weird I know. You here, me here in a town that doesn't' exist. You got family, friends, a job you need to get back to and I'm the only one that can get you back. Now I'm telling it to you straight and you better take it on faith that I'm telling it straight or you'll never get back, and that's the honest truth."

Norman slipped into the sweat suit—one size fits all, but the high-topped gym shoes were at least two sizes too large. As he drew the laces tight he surveyed the room. Except for two basketball hoops without nets it was empty. A dark circle and a series of dark squares on the wall bore mute testimony to the previous existence of a clock and pictures.

"Well, you're ready. Pretty good fit huh?"

"I want to make a phone call. I'm allowed one under the law. I want to make it now," Norman said.

"Yeah, you're allowed a phone call and I'd be glad to oblige but we don't have any phones here. Besides you're not being held against your will or nothing. You're not being booked, you're not even in jail. Think about that. You're free as a bird only you can't go anywhere until you sober up. I'm the only way out of here 'cause I'm the only one that knows the timing of the exit. I only know about getting you out, I don't know nothing about getting in."

Sheriff Mann began a slow jog and motioned Norman to follow. As they moved around the floor a jumble of thoughts crowded Norman's consciousness. Nothing was right here. It was like everything was turned back fifty years. The inlaid maple floor creaked ominously with each step, and the heavy, moisture laden air made breathing difficult. His feet felt as if they were sloshing around in the over-sized shoes. He had once seen a similar pair in the museum with George Mikan's name on them. It was eerie. A shiver went down his spine led there by a rivulet of sweat.

"Pick it up bud, we got to get it going."

The Sheriff was running backwards and talking in Norman's face. Each time Norman picked up the pace he stayed right there exhorting him to even greater exertion. Several laps later Norman's legs ached and his breathing had become labored.

"We'll slow down, let you get your wind back."

The sweat-soaked shirt hung heavy and limp and reeked of bourbon. With each step cold air billowed beneath it and he shivered. The air was stifling and moisture laden and Norman found it difficult to catch his breath. Finally, when he was wheezing the Sheriff called a halt.

Slowly, Norman's breathing returned to normal. He bent over, hands on his knees, watching huge droplets of sweat puddle on the floor between his floppy gym shoes. That's when he spied something shiny stuck in the mud between the boards. It looked like a coin, but before he could inspect it he was hit in the side with a large ball.

"Dodge ball, bud. Remember how it was in grade school? You're it."

The Sheriff and his deputy kept Norman moving all around the gym. His quick starts and turns threatened to take him out of his ill-fitting shoes. He could feel blisters forming on the balls of his feet. He was becoming sober and his reflexes were returning as he made the two policemen miss more often. He was even getting into the spirit of the game, which surprised him at his competitiveness.

"OK, time," the Sheriff said. "We been at this for more than three hours, let's see how you're doing."

Norman was instructed to close his eyes and touch his nose. He walked the foul line several times and never wavered.

"I think you're ready for a swim and a shower," the Sheriff said. The pool was small, maybe thirty feet in length, and the water was a brownish color.

"Last one in's a tar baby," Joe Mann said and shoved Norman into the pool. The water was warm and foul smelling like the punky, putrid water found in rotten tree stumps. Norman had no place to put the coin except in his mouth. He was sure the sheriff would take it away if he knew.

Despite the drag of the heavy sweat suit Norman managed to swim several laps. When it seemed he could no longer continue the Sheriff called a halt.

"You want to keep on?"

Norman could only shake his head no.

"Well, we still got a few minutes to play with, but if you've had it the shower's over yonder," the Sheriff said, pointing to the far end of the gym.

From somewhere distant the water pipes shuddered and with each shudder the showerhead sputtered and threatened to stop. The rusty colored water was brackish and tasted like tannic acid. He took the coin out and washed them under the shower. It had an engraving of Liberty on one side and the other had a wreath enclosing three I's. After wiping it dry it became clear it was Roman Numerals for the number three. It was dated 1882. It might be some kind of token for a school fundraiser. In any case it was simply the only tangible thing he had so he decided to keep it.

His left shoe had something in the toe that had bounced around and irritated his big toe. He shook it and finally had to unlace it to retrieve a rusty button with remnants of paint with a big I on the first line and on the second a LI and the third a KE.

Norman wiped dry and the questions that had been forming in his mind surfaced. Now he intended to get some answers. If he did perhaps he wouldn't sue, but then again maybe he would. Somebody was going to pay for his mistreatment.

Joe Mann brought in a plate of country ham and eggs. "You earned this, bud," he said and left abruptly.

Norman couldn't remember when he'd ever been so hungry. He wolfed down the ham and eggs and wished he had a cup of coffee to go with it.

"Your car's ready, let's go!"

Norman tried to request a phone call, but the sheriff was already out the door.

"You can't make a phone call. There's no phones. You can't send a telegram. Same reason. There's only five people in this town and you've met 'em all. Now do you want to stay here with us or go home?"

"Sheriff, you can't violate my rights like that. I'm entitled to one phone call and I want to make it now."

Joe Mann opened Norman's car door and with a flourish of his left hand invited Norman to sit.

"That answer your question? If you shut up and keep moving you'll be out of here in a few minutes. Then you can make all the phone calls you want. Now what'll it be? Stay or go?"

Norman turned the key, the engine started and he felt reassured and in touch with something familiar and solid.

He slowly followed the 1946 Ford as it wound its way up the mountain road in the dense fog. The Sheriff applied his brakes.

"This is it, bud. Just a few more feet and you're over the hill and on your way. I hope your little stay here has been useful and you learn to stay off the booze from now on. If no, I'll be waiting."

The Sheriff made a quick U-turn and as his tail lights disappeared in the fog Norman quietly said "It hasn't been fun Sheriff Joe Mann, but we'll meet again I'm sure."

Norman sat there a few minutes to get his bearings when he sensed a lightening, a thinning of the fog. He gunned the engine and in a few feet he has in the clear and headed down the mountain. The air was delightfully free of moisture and it smelled of freedom. Norman breathed so deeply that he became light-headed.

He came to a small town and pulled into a diagonal parking spot outside the Town Hall, Post Office and Police Station.

He relayed the story to the deputy on duty, who wrote it all down. When Norman finished the deputy gave him a querulous glance and called the duty sergeant.

The sergeant looked Norman over from head to toe before uttering a word.

"You'd better come in my office," he said, opening a swinging gate to let Norman enter. As they sat down the Sergeant put his hands behind his head and took a long time before speaking.

"Son, you're the fourth person that's told me this story in the fifteen years I've been on the force. Now I'm going to tell you what I told them. Daisy don't exist. Hasn't ever since the dam was finished back in the fifties. As for the people you said you met, they've been dead just as long. Now Joe Mann, his deputy Clarence Mullins and the three men you said you saw in the bar:

Woodrow W. Ratliff, Casimir Adkins and J. T. Stambaugh don't have a good reputation around here."

The Sergeant looked at the ceiling for a few seconds as if collecting his thoughts and then looked Norman in the eye and asked, "Are you a reporter?"

Norman replied in the negative.

Well, then I'll give you a quick background. The rest you can get from the court records if you want to know more. If you were a reporter you could get your own damn information. I'm sick of talking to that bunch, always looking for a new angle on an old story."

He leaned forward on his desk and looked at Norman's report.

"Oh! Yeah. I see here you're a computer consultant. Maybe you could help us with ours, the damned thing seems to have a mind of its own. But I'll bet you're not interested in that are you?"

Norman didn't respond.

"Where was I?" the Sergeant asked rhetorically, "Oh! Yeah! The story of them five boys. It was the night before the dam gates was to be closed. They went down there and got drunk in Woodrow's bar and went tearing through town in that souped up patrol car of Joe's. All the residents and businesses had been moved out and the boys was having a grand old time. Yessir! A grand old time before the town disappeared under 70 feet of water. Now nobody was supposed to be there unless they had permission from the Corps of Engineers. Well, it seems they did give permission to a group of school kids to have a flag lowering ceremony at their school. Only they died before they got there. Joe Mann and his drunken buddies hit the bus full broadside setting it on fire: Twenty two of the thirty five members of the choir were killed along with all five in the car. They didn't find hardly a thing from the car, only a couple of melted belt buckles and some pocket change."

"But what about these things I found?" Norman handed the items to the Sergeant.

"Well, son. This don't prove nothing except you found some old stuff. I do remember something from back then. Let me check the records."

He pulled a couple of tired looking folders from a file drawer in the back of the small office.

"Yep, here it is. They was having a show and tell back then and Geraldine Mooney lost a three-cent nickel she had taken from her dad's collection. It was worth a few bucks so they shut the school down for a day while they did a sweep. Never found it."

"But this thing looks more like a dime to me. Let me see if our computer will work long enough to check it out. If not I can call somebody

When he reached the top of the mountain the fog had lifted and the view was breathtaking. Stretching out for miles in every direction was a patchwork quilt of farms, houses and fields. A lake shimmered in the hot morning sun and the dam shone white in the brilliant sunlight.

The route down from his vantage point was back the way he had come from Daisy. Now there was only a circular tourist lookout and a rest area.

Norman searched for evidence of the road, but the trees and underbrush looked pristine and undisturbed.

It promised to be a hot and stifling autumn day. Norman sat down on the guardrail. His side ached and his feet hurt. A ribbon of sweat formed on his upper lip. The motion of wiping it dry irritated his side. He lifted his shirt to reveal a large, volleyball-sized bruise. His socks appeared stuck as he carefully peeled them off to discover large blisters on the balls of both feet.

Norman, now filled with resolve, headed back toward the Sergeant with his new evidence. Now maybe they wouldn't make wild accusations about too much moonshine and wild parties. When he reached the turn-off for the Interstate, however, he fingered the coin for a few seconds of indecision and then turned west—toward home.

An Unexamined Life

When I was growing up, I spent every summer on my grandparent's farm in eastern Kentucky. My grandfather was a prolific storyteller (a trade practiced and polished before the red-glowing pot-bellied stove in his father's store) and he told me stories about the people, living and dead, but mostly dead, who had once lived in the area. Many of the names he mentioned I found carved on headstones in family graveyards that dotted the hilltops.

I loved the old farmhouse with its colonnaded porch wrapped L shaped around the side; I loved the smell of dried hay in the barn and of corn in the crib, and yet I always felt that Kentucky was more dead than alive, at least the eastern Appalachian area. I walked through once cultivated fields and learned to wear protection against saw briars, dewberries and other stickers that loved open ground. My trips also uncovered foundations of former residences now marked by orange-throated Tiger lilies.

My morbidity was not my grandfather's fault. He was concerned with colorful stories about the dead, and he lived comfortably in the drama of his memory; everything was continually in the present to him My grandmother occasionally became poetic but not enough to influence me. She was in the latter stages of untreated diabetes and often followed her rhapsodic recollections with paranoiac accusations. The summer I turned fourteen I saw her dying, bedridden and gangrenous for one whole summer, yet my own mourning for the dead and the past had begun even earlier.

Many of my grandfather's stories were symptomatic, to me not him, of Kentucky's decay. A story might include a road now impassable because of new growth, or a barn or outbuilding whose foundations now sported head high weeds.

I accepted many of the characters in my grandfather's stories by valuing them differently from him. So many of them had lived unfilled lives. He often talked about Kenus Salisbury, a distant relative. I knew Kenus well, yet the image I retained of him was a combination of what my grandfather had told me and what I had observed. Kenus was the last of that particular breed produced by frontier conditions and innate, though uncultivated, engineering abilities. He made handles for every tool on the farm so there were many cues to remind my grandfather of him. Most of the stories were funny, for Kenus was eccentric. Yet when my laughter died, the final effect of the stores was not funny. Kenus became for me the symbol of a dying place.

Every spring, when I appeared, he always stopped by with a tow bag full of popcorn on the cob. The bag always contained more than a bushel of the five-fingered cobs bristling with rows of flinty, red kernels. He grew it especially for me and I was his only customer. I still have some of the best cobs strung up and hanging in my den. They look like shrunken hands severed at the wrist.

I loved Kenus and I felt his affection for me, but when I thought of the malady that afflicted eastern Kentucky I always thought of it in terms of red, five-fingered corn cobs and the wasted potential of Kenus Salisbury.

I have seen pictures of Kenus as a young man. He was tall and lean of body, with thick wrists and huge hands that seemed attached to the wrong body. He was not handsome. He had an angular face in which two eyes peered out that could pierce metal. I remember him as old. When I first met him he must have been about sixty-five. The image I retained has him bent slightly from the waist and to the left, so that he walked sidewise like a crab, with his crooked left hand, wrapped in a red stocking, held tightly to his breast.

Kenus went to Cincinnati to work in a factory when he was about twenty. An accident mangled his left hand and left it bent like the crook on a shepherd's staff. He returned home, bought a few acres of land and retired. He lived alone, with few ventures into the world, for more than forty years until he died.

Kenus was a hard worker, skillful but slow. The best thing about him was his pride in good work, but he often didn't know when to stop. He was not interested in your problems, but in the problems of the job itself. A pile of rusted mower blades attested to his tenacity. He had worked them to razor sharpness and then spent two more weeks shaping and sharpening them to his specifications. He wore out every file and whetstone my grandfather had and sent into town for a new supply. In the meantime, anxious to get his hay in, my grandfather bought a new set and finished his mowing.

I knew Kenus to shoe a horse, dig a well, build a barn, make smoking pipes out of soapstone, whittle countless hundreds of hickory tool handles, roof buildings with split oak shingles and construct a rudimentary Archimedes screw to irrigate his garden. In the winter he often spent his days constructing split-oak baskets, which were sturdy and strong.

When he was young he must have been nearly self-sufficient. He would refuse outside jobs. He paid his property taxes by hewing railroad ties from oak logs, for which the railroad paid four dollars. In the winter evenings he polished hickory handles with a piece of broken glass; some for work around the farm and some for trade.

For food he had his vegetables and the game he trapped plus the increase of his small chicken flock. He needed little in the way of clothes. About the only item he ever bought besides "overhawls" were red stockings for his left hand and for his feet. He canned hundreds of jars of carrots, tomatoes, beans, corn, peas and fruit on his small stove. His wild blackberry jam was best I've ever tasted.

A new hard-topped road built after World War II destroyed his tool handle business. Farmers found they could go to town and be back with a new handle in the time it took to explain their needs to Kenus. The new changes brought about by faster communication with the world bothered him not a whit. He had other problems. Rural electrification was moving apace and the local electric company wanted to plant a pole in the middle of his property. Kenus fought them all that summer. He often spent the entire day atop the ridge when work crews were in the area. In the end he lost out, but he never subscribed to their service.

Kenus spent years terracing his property and he never forgave the electric company for planting that creosoted abomination right in the middle of it. About twenty feet below the crest of the hill he built a retaining wall of Black Locust logs. He then slowly began scraping the dirt down until he completed the first terrace. He dug a little too deep around the utility pole and some of the dirt had to be replaced to keep it from falling. He then moved down the hill and built another terrace. He said the Chinese had been doing it for 5,000 years. It worked for them and he was "dang shure hit would work fer him."

He wasted nothing. As soon as an area was level he seeded. Corn was planted in at least a dozen places. It was of varying heights and interspersed with other vegetables. He carried two buckets on either end of a stout stick, and he arranged with farmers to pick up cow pies from their pastures and barns. He buried newspapers for mulch and fertilizer. One of the strangest sights I witnessed was a walking cardboard box. Kenus had punched holes in it, upended it over his head and started for home. There he patiently ripped it into pieces and buried it in the garden.

In the years I knew him he always wore the same uniform: Blue heavy denims with the high bib in front and faded almost white at the knees. In the summer he went shirtless; in the winter he wore an ancient wool shirt so heavily patched and stitched that the material almost disappeared. Over this he wore a light brown, heavy overcoat with rope ties where the buttons used to be.

Kenus built his shack astride Frank's creek to eliminate the need for an outhouse, or as he termed, "house of office." While he considered his personal needs he ignored the needs of Frank's creek. One rainy spring, three years after he settled in, the creek rose and carried his shack several hundred feet downstream. My grandfather told me it was rumored that some of Kenus' peaches floated all the way to New Orleans.

He rebuilt his shack ten feet above the creek on poles sunk to bedrock. The only entrance was by way of a semi-circular stairway of logs. "That creek ain't a' gonna warsh me out no more," he said with finality.

Over they years the shack grew smaller. Layers of canned goods grew inward until Kenus could barely move around. It wasn't that he was miserly, but in times of plenty he canned everything and just didn't get around to eating it.

In the summer he slept on the small porch, upright in a cane bottomed chair; in winter he curled up on a pallet of quilts. A tiny path among the canned goods led from the front door to his small stove and back to the hole in the floor. The ceiling and walls were insulated with layers of magazines and pages from seed catalogues held there by flour paste. One section of the ceiling was covered with a 1936 edition of Grit magazine. I stood there trying to read it, but hurt my neck. Kenus noticed and rearranged his inventory so I could lie on the floor and read my magazine in comfort. At that distance, however, I couldn't make out the letters, but I never let him know.

I spent many delightful summer evenings on the small porch. The musical notes of Frank's creek often lulled me to sleep, and I used to lie there wishing it could always be like that. We would sit there, saying nothing, comfortable in each other's company. Then about 9 P. M. Kenus would announce his bedtime. I always had just enough twilight left to make it home to my grandfather's. I could hear Kenus snore before I reached the bottom of the stairs.

Besides canned goods, Kenus had a complete selection of hickory handles of all kinds, all hand carved and no two exactly alike. He carved every one from a set of specifications in his head. As he worked he hummed and tunelessly whistled hymns. His favorite was "Swing Low Sweet Chariot."

He once spent several weeks fitting a handle for one of the church elders. The elder complained that two dollars was too much to pay for a handle that could be bought in town for a dollar fifty. He offered Kenus one dollar for the job. Kenus refused to take anything and never went to church again. If an elder cheated then the church couldn't be trusted. He hummed his hymns and read his bible alone.

Chickens provided a ready source of income. In the summer they laid eggs all over the place because Kenus didn't have the heart to pen them up.

I spent hours searching for nests; I got to keep half. I traded mine for candy, gum and bags of Stud smoking tobacco. Kenus took his half in cash, which he stored in a Clabber Girl baking powder can. There was only one problem that I could see with the arrangement. The hens were setting, hatching the eggs, and some of the eggs I found had half-formed chickens inside. They all went to the store. I often wondered who ate the immature chickens.

Kenus never smoked and didn't have any vices that I was aware of, though he did own up to chewing a little Strater's Natural Leaf now and then. I smoked, or at least was learning to, but Kenus never admonished me for it. It simply didn't matter to him, and he let me stash my tobacco in a small niche beside the door. When he delivered my supply of popcorn each spring he slyly let me know my smoking supplies were still intact.

Tending a garden on top of a small hill presented problems. After several successive dry summers and hauling buckets of water Kenus decided to irrigate. He began construction of what I later learned was an Archimedes screw. First he built a huge vise of logs to hold the work steady and began drilling. Soon he had hollowed out a three-foot length of poplar log. Then he began work on the screw. The work carried over into the winter and was still in progress the next spring when I arrived. He had patiently whittled and polished the edges of the screw until it was smooth as glass. He inserted into the hollowed log and it fit perfectly. He stepped back and triumphantly clapped his hands and danced a little jig. "Boys," he said as if I had somehow multiplied myself into a crowd, "this here's the most perfect thing I have done."

Well, it was too perfect and the red oak from which it was constructed swelled up with water and refused to turn. Kenus laid the screw up to dry and concentrated on hauling water to his garden by hand.

A year later that screw worked to perfection. Apparently Kenus had modified his original and a few minutes of cranking irrigated the entire garden through a series of hollowed out half-logs. Needless to say the garden responded with some of the largest produce Kenus had ever seen. That was the year he miscalculated and planted 144 tomato plants. My grandfather said he should have named the place "Rotten Tomato Lane."

Viewed from the road that ran past the mouth of Frank's creek, Kenus garden looked like birthday cake with one brown, skinny candle on top.

The same road that destroyed his handle business also destroyed his privacy. Had he been of a different mold he would have capitalized On it by charging admission. Money didn't matter to him. What did matter was that he cared about people keeping their word; he cared about honor. The first year or two he loaded down gawkers with homegrown produce. He would take nothing in exchange. His laconic reply was, "Hit cost me nothin'."

Some people came from town to view the exhibit as if it was their right. Finally, Kenus gave up trying to tend his garden when a group of screaming cub scouts invaded his place.

In exasperation he planted the entire hill in sunflowers. "Let 'em come and see that," he said, and moved into one of my grandfather's upstairs bedrooms.

Many people did come to see "Sunflower Hill." In the fall, after everyone went home, birds came to gorge on the seeds. And now that Kenus wasn't there to protect it the groundhogs, field mice and other small animals avenged their ancestors by nibbling away at everything edible.

I saw Kenus shortly before he died in 1952. His eyes still burned with that inner fire. He told me there was a poke of popcorn hanging by the door, and he gestured toward the shack. I noticed he had on a new red stocking. Other than that it was just like all the other times, yet seeing him ready to die I was impressed by the wasted body, lying frail beneath a new nightgown.

Was it just wasted potential—that energy, that ingenuity, that strength to do what he wanted that symbolized his life to me?

Kenus lived a full life if three score years and ten can be called full. He worked hard at being himself, but when he died it was as if he never existed.

Shortly after his death I visited his property for the last time. It revealed none of the residue I expected from Kenus's life. Strip miners had cut a huge gash across the beautiful countryside I had known. Its innards had been shamelessly exposed by a diesel shovel capable of moving as much dirt in one scoop as Kenus had in an entire year.

Kenus shack lay buried somewhere beneath tons of overburden that had been dumped in Frank's creek, which no longer ran in the summer. Huge, ugly gashes marked the vicious path on its various rampages during times of rain. Now there was a hole in the ground deeper than the hill had been high. Kicking the ground in anger at the sacrilege committed against this beautiful land my foot struck something. When I wiped the dirt off I saw it was one of Kenus' handles. I still have it today beside the shrunken hands—a broken axe handle; symbol of an unexamined life.

The Restaurant Code Cracked

My wife and I received an unexpected dividend. It wasn't enough to make us independently wealthy, but it was enough for a good dinner or a new bowling ball. My wife decided we should go to a small, elegant restaurant she had heard about. I argued for a new bowling ball and a trip to Cracker Barrel. We argued, not vehemently, for several days until I thought I had won. I deposited the check and went to the local pro shop to look over the new balls. She smiled politely and seemed to be totally happy with the decision.

The next day we went to the little restaurant. I should have known I was in over my head when the waiter appeared with a little white towel over his arm. From then on I didn't understand a thing he described to us. Waiters always walk you through the menu with a fluidity and grace that comes only with intimate association with the menu.

"Tonight," he intoned, "we have parsella of poulan smothered in a rich sauce of steamed sea parkels, served on a bed of browned rice and fresh herbs picked from Chef Pierre's own garden. This is baked on our two-shovel casserole for twelve minutes and then it's layered with beggarworm and wagnot leaves—very exclusive.

"We also offer," and here he paused and intoned, as if in reverence, "Chef Pierre's specialty: A triple rack of riblets, drizzled with a blasticon of buri buri sauce. This is then gently placed in a chiminea and allowed to sweat until tender under a blanket of rhubarb leaves and sun-ripened asphalt." My wife is not fazed at all by this strange terminology.

She wades in trying to keep the bewildering array of options separate.

"Is it the Megadillo that's grilled and presented on a bed of spelt?"

"Oh. No. That's the sautéed monkling," our waiter said. "The Megadillo comes with a side of greens on a bed of Genninfelters. It is then tossed with cold expressed Buckeye oil and allowed to gently cook in its own juices."

She keeps on but most of this stuff I would never eat, except, perhaps, after imbibing a whole lot of bourbon.

For his part, the waiter kept presenting us with descriptions of roulades, timbales, frittatas, legumbres en pipian with parsellas and other strange concoctions. "Just bring me something that once breathed," I started to say, but my wife had her foot drawn back and aimed at my shin. I have a discoloration there from the last time she stabbed me with her stileto-toed shoe, so I kept my silence and my outward show of civility.

Finally, the waiter finished his performance with something that sounded like "Ochos Rios cutlets and watermelon seeds."

"Did Chef Pierre have to club it?" I asked. The pained look on my wife's face pointed out that she had hooked her shoe on the chair rung and I escaped severe pain by the thinnest of margins.

"Do you have anything that once belonged to a pig?" I moved my legs sideways and she kicked the chair rungs.

"Certainly sir. We can offer a nice spread of pork cutlets raised by our maitre de and carved by him from the flank of a pig from our own farm right here on the river. This is marinated in a delightful and aromatic mixture of fresh herbs and hop Hornbeam bark."

"Is that pork chops cut right from a real hog?" I asked.

"Not a term we care to use sir, but yes it comes from a real hog."

He wiped his hands several times on the white towel and inspected them to see if they were dirtied by his use of such a common phrase.

I warmed to the task. There was real food to be had here once one knew the language.

"Well, I'll take it," I said confidently. "And I'd like with incarcerated potatoes, concomited vegetables and a glass of wine, preferably red, served chilled and transported to my table on a tray of ambergris and incense. I had no idea what the last meant, but the waiter did. He nodded as he wrote down my order, clearly impressed that I had figured out the menu. He straightened up, did a right face and disappeared.

"And no parsellas," I told him. I may be unschooled when it comes to fancy food, but one thing I know for sure, I don't want any parsellas with my pork chops.

Some Soap

Some months ago before the National Do Not Call list was active I received telephone calls from solicitors for every conceivable item. Always they seemed to time them for the dinner meal. Often I hung up and groused about how I should call them at their dinnertime and see how they liked it.

It seems one can never think of the proper, witty *coup de grace* to a sales pitch. The next day, however, one can think of two or three really good put-downs when it's too late. Some months back I got it right. I answered the phone, during dinner, of course, and this young telemarketer said he was calling from Salt Lake City. He went on to detail how the Mormons supported his earth friendly products.

As the pitch became clear I was the winner of a Cadillac, $7500 cash or a Hawaiian holiday. I asked how I won and he said their computer picked me. I queried him again and he backed up to a contest he said I entered several years ago. Anyway he said it didn't matter, I was a winner and he needed an address to which the prize could be sent, after we took care of some business.

It seems I couldn't take delivery of my prize until I bought some biodegradable soap endorsed by the Tabernacle Choir. The cost to me was just $300. Usually at this point I would hang up the phone, but I had the presence of mind to ask for the Cadillac. He, of course, replied he wasn't authorized to disburse prizes but would ask his manager as soon as I bought the soap. Now I wasn't about to buy six quarts of ecclesiastical soap. I don't think I've used that much soap since I was born. Anyway I repeated my offer, that if they would send me the Cadillac and I liked it, liked it a lot; then I would buy the heavenly soap.

He reiterated his offer just as he was trained to do in telemarketing boot camp. This was to ensure I hadn't misinterpreted the offer, which I hadn't. Then he intoned in his most authoritative voice that it was a bona fide offer and I indeed was a winner—guaranteed as soon as I gave them my credit card number and bought the celestial soap. In fact he would have his office manager deliver the Cadillac right to my door if I won.

Now he became conditional on me, he had never used the IF word before. So I repeated my original offer, "Send me the Cadillac, which I've already won, and if I like it I'll take two orders of your green, earth friendly soap and I'll get my neighbor, who has horses to order some too." Then I added, "Do you want to buy a horse? I use my neighbor's manure on my garden every year and it makes things really green—like your soap." My young tormentor lost his composure and consigned me to the nether regions of the earth. His parting words were, "Well, I guess I'll have to find someone more intelligent." He hung up before I could agree.

A Lost Wallet

Jamie met Duny Gene by accident. The semi-annual visit of the Collins-McGraw carnival was one of the recreational highlights of the year in North Matewan, West Virginia. Each spring the carnival stopped on its northward migration and reversed the process each fall as it headed back toward its winter quarters in Florida.

Against the gaudy and raucous midway Duny Gene spied a lonely, disconsolate figure. Jamie, his hands thrust so deeply in his pockets they formed lumps on each thigh, his shoulders hunched until they almost met in front, stood in stark contrast to the fun-loving crowd around him.

Something about the dejected figure attracted Duny Gene. Jamie shuffled slowly, head down, his feet making gouges in the sawdust, leaving scars where the dry, brown grass peeked through.

"Why're you lookin' so punk buddy? Duny gene said. "Didja lose somethin'?"

Startled, Jamie looked up. "Do...do I know you?"

"We ain't never done nothin' together, classes and all that, but I seen you around."

Jamie didn't reply.

"Look. I'm Duny, Duny Gene Mooney. You're Jamie aint'cha?" When Jamie failed to respond he said, " Hey you looked like you needed help that's all. See you around."

The need for companionship overcame Jamie's reserve and as Duny Gene turned to go he found his voice. "Wait. I could use some help I guess. I've lost my wallet around here somewhere."

Together they retraced Jamie's route from one end of the carnival to the other.

"There ain't enough sawdust here to hide a pencil eraser let alone a wallet. Somebody has already found it," Duny Gene said.

"You're probably right. Maybe we should start asking some of these people.

"Yeah. Who? Look round here. You gonna ask all these people?" "Well, I don't know. If someone found my wallet don't you think they'd want to return it if they knew I was looking for it?"

"Boy, you sure are..." Duny Gene caught himself before had added the word dumb. "You sure want that wallet back real bad don'tcha. Didja have any money in it?"

"Not much. Maybe three dollars, I just want it back. It's brand new and my grandmother gave it to me and I've got Joe Dimaggio's picture in it and..."

Tears had formed in Jamie's eyes and his chin began to quiver. Duny Gene couldn't stand such weakness.

"Let's ask him to make an announcement," Duny Gene said, pointing toward the Two Headed Baby tent where the operator was cajoling the crowd with a bullhorn. They explained the situation and after the operator determined Jamie's whereabouts at the carnival he leaned forward and in an authoritative yet conspiratorial voice he told them to get a policeman and return to the Silver Bullet. He went on to explain that they tried to run a clean show, but those two crooks made them all look dirty. Before they left he swore them to silence about his part. "I never told you a thing. You just do like I said. But I never told you, you got it?"

They turned to go and the operator asked, "Say how much money did you have in it?" When Jamie indicated three dollars the operator beckoned them to come closer. "Look boys, you'll do a lot of us a favor if you come up with a large amount. Say something like thirty dollars or so. You'll get it or they'll go to jail. Now move and mum's the word, right?"

When they were a short way from the tent Jamie said, "We can't just walk over there and call them thieves can we?"

"We sure can," Duny Gene said. "I say we do unless you got a better idea."

"But it's not right. I mean I can't do that to those guys, besides how do we know if that Two Headed Baby man is trying to get even for something?"

"We don't, but I sure did like his idea. Didn't you?"

Duny Gene had had a run in with the two operators of the Silver Bullet last time the carnival was in town. They had cleaned him out on the Wheel of Fortune, and now he saw his chance to get even. "I'll tell you what, I'll buy us an RC and a hot dog and we can go up on the tracks to think it over OK?"

From the vantage point Duny Gene chose they could see the entire carnival. "Looks kinda small from here don't it?"

"Sure is," Jamie said between bites. "Thanks for the hot dog. I was really hungry."

"I always think better after I eat. Just look at that carnival. Why it's stuck there between Big Stinkin' Creek and the track here. Don't you wish you could pick up the creek and the track between two big peaveys and snap them together and squeeze the carnival up tight, why I'd bet your wallet'd pop out real quick like. Like squeezin' a papaw until the seeds come out the end. That'd be somethin' wouldn't it?"

"Yeah," said Jamie responding to the fantasy. "Maybe we could fly over the whole thing in a space ship with a big vacuum cleaner and suck everything up until we found the wallet."

"That'd be the easy thing to do...

"What's a peavey?" Jamie interrupted.

"Why it's a pole with a hook on one end they use to roll logs with." "Roll logs huh."

Duny Gene had stretched out full length. Jamie sat on the rail, his headcupped in his hands. Neither spoke for several minutes. The sounds of the crowd and the rides were muted, but a rendition of "It's a Grand Night for Singing" came through loud and clear. At this distance the carnival was less threatening, especially the Silver Bullet where Jamie could see the cars making their metallic arcs against the night sky.

Something about Duny Gene attracted Jamie. Maybe it was his congenial way of ingratiating himself in such a short time that Jamie felt they had been friends for a long time_ Perhaps it was his free spirited ways that promised to reveal experiences and adventures Jamie only dreamed about.

"Say, look at them stars," Duny gene said. He looked at the night sky and continued, "you can see the Big Dipper, and Orion, and Cassyopie or whatever they call it. Why I'd bet if we didn't have all those lights from the carnival shinin' up we could see just about ever' constellation we learned about in school. He turned to Jamie, "I think we oughta go right down there and get your money.

You can see the policeman standing right there beside the gate. Whatta you say?"

"I'm not sure. I can't walk up to those two guys and call them crooked. It's not fair to them."

"Look, Jamie. Life ain't fair If you want to win you gotta take chances.

Now you gotta act like you're cocksure, like little banty roosters. Ain't bigger'n a minute but they get their share because they crow louder and longer. Now if we go down there and they ain't got the wallet all you have to do is start cryin' like you just lost your dog and I'll grab you and we'll walk off real quick."

"I'm still not sure."

"Well, think about it while we walk down there. we gotta go get it, 'cause not to would be worse than lettin' them keep it. It just ain't right lettin' that fat guy and his rat-faced buddy walk out of here with our money. Besides if we go down there and they got a whole box full of stuff they stole we'd be heroes or somethin' Maybe even get a reward."

"Yeah, but it isn't our money it's my money."

"Why, sure. I just thought if we got a lot of money from those guys maybe we could split it. Ain't that fair?"

"Yeah, I guess so."

That sounded like tacit agreement to Duny Gene's ears and he quickly grabbed Jamie and headed back toward the carnival.

Near the entrance the policeman stood swinging his nightstick out of boredom. When Jamie spied him he lost his courage. Duny Gene lifted him by the arm and led him forward all the while talking in his ear. "Look," Duny gene said in a lowered voice, "You don't have to say a thing unless you want to. Let me do all the talkin' and don't say anything that goes against what I say. All you gotta do is nod your head from time to time. You can still do that can't you?"

Jamie's mouth was too dry for speech and there was no cooperation at all between his lips and tongue. As if that wasn't bad enough he had the ashen pallor of a one being led to his execution. He shivered so violently it appeared every muscle was out of control, and he walked with a stiff legged gait. As they drew close to the Silver Bullet Jamie became a real drag, because his legs had become so out of control he looked like the scarecrow in "Wizard of Oz." They were several steps behind the policeman, who stopped to wait for them. Duny Gene, tired of dragging the reluctant Jamie, propped him up against a tent pole.

After making an excuse about Jamie's upset stomach they closed the distance to the Silver Bullet. Just the sight of the policeman walking up frightened the fatman, who turned to run and tripped over a guy wire. When fatman regained his footing the policeman poked his three cell flashlight a foot deep in fatman's ample belly, and inquired about the missing wallet.

Jamie could see the gestures and guess as to what was being said. When fatman looked at

Duny Gene and shook his head no, Jamie broke wind, wet his pants and almost lost his grip on the tent pole. Then the policeman stabbed the air with his flashlight and pointed it straight toward Jamie, who felt the draft from the Avenging Angel's wings and with a loud groan sank slowly to the ground.

Jamie's groan dissolved and merged with the noises of the carnival. Unknown to Jamie, his collapse was just about perfect. The policeman put his face right into fatman's so that his words were not lost, "You see how sick that boy is? Now you got about ten seconds to cough up that wallet or you won't be standing here long."

Fatman's eyes scurried about his face like scared rats trapped in a silo. He licked his suddenly dry lips, tried to hitch his pants past his protruding belly and

nervously fiddled with his belt buckle with two hammy hands. When it appeared he might join Jamie in discomfiture, his cohort, rat-faced man, came striding up with a solicitous smile on his face as he waved Jamie's billfold in the air. The constable snatched the wallet away for his hand and turned to Duny Gene for identification. Jamie watched from the corner of his eye as Duny Gene held the wallet up to display Joe Dimaggio's picture.

Like a film of a train wreck played backwards, Jamie's uncooperative body parts, which just seconds ago had exhibited no memory of each other, suddenly came together and he found he could stand and walk. He took a few halting steps and faced fatman.

"This your wallet son?" the policeman asked.

Jamie took the wallet and checked the pictures and showed the policeman his Social Security card. "I know the number by heart sir," he said. The sir came out something like shir because his saliva had not resumed its flow.

"OK, let me hear it."

Jamie recited the number, his voice rising as his confidence grew.

The policeman then opened the wallet to reveal its emptiness. He tilted toward Fatman with a questioning look on his face. Fatman just shook his head.

All the while he had been as unwitting a participant as one could find. All the questions had been directed at him, yet he never left the gate. He really didn't know if there had been money in the wallet. He turned toward rat-faced man and held his hands out in supplication and shrugged his shoulders. Rat-faced man shook his head and made a gesture with his hand that said zero.

The policeman turned to Jamie and said, "Well son?"

Before Jamie could frame a reply Duny Gene said, "We had thirty-four dollars in there."

"Didn't you tell me it was his wallet?"

"Well...yeah...you see," Duny Gene hesitantly replied, "he was carrying my money too."

"And the two of you had thirty-four dollars?"

"Yes sir!" Duny Gene said with finality.

Jamie stood dumbstruck. He was unprepared for such a turn of events and it was all he could do to nod dumbly. The policeman studied each boy in turn for several seconds and satisfied that they might have that much money he turned and motioned rat-faced man to him. "All right boys let's have it, thirty-four dollars."

Terrified, Jamie was incapable of movement or he would have taken off. He watched in amazement as the two shady operators scrambled to put together the money. The policeman offered his hat as a repository and the pile of crumpled bills nearly filled it up. Thirty-four dollars was a good week's wages in 1947 and certainly it was a lot for two fourteen-year-old boys to have. When it appeared the two didn't have any more money Duny Gene worried that he had guessed too high. They watched as the policeman counted out loud, "That's thirty-three dollars and twenty-seven cents. Is that OK with you boys?" he asked with a smile on his face. They agreed to the amount and Duny Gene stuffed the bills in his pocket.

At the gate Duny Gene seemed to take an eternity expressing his thanks for the policeman's help. Jamie could see deliverance immediately at hand in the circle of diffused light outside the carnival and just beyond it--blackness.

"Let's go back up on the tracks, we gotta figure out what to do."

Jamie needed no further encouragement and took off like a freed bird. He ran straight through a copse of sumac saplings, jumped a six foot drainage ditch and cleared a path through a patch of head-high pigweed. When he reached the tracks he looked back and through eyes welled up with tears he could just make out the Two Headed Baby show and it appeared they had a smile on their faces.